This Little Tiger book belongs to:

Brooke

Sure enough, there was a delicious-looking dragonfly. Harry was just about to jump when . . .

. . . the dragonfly flew off, high
into the air.
"You can't eat me!" she called.
"I'm much too quick for you."

Harry was wondering
what to do next when
suddenly he saw . . .

. . . a big juicy caterpillar
on a twig above him.

"Goody, goody,
dinner at last!" cried
Harry, but when he flicked
out his long tongue to
catch it . . .

. . . the caterpillar
laughed. "You can't
eat me!" she said.
"My hairs would
tickle your tongue."

"Never mind, I'll find something soon," said Harry.
He bounced on until he met . . .

. . . a scrumptious-looking snail crawling towards him.

"Yummy, yummy," said Harry, but when he reached it . . .

. . . the snail's head suddenly disappeared!
"You can't eat me!" said the
snail from inside its shell.
"I'm much too clever."

Harry was getting hungrier and hungrier.
He was just about to give up and go
home to his mum, when he spotted . . .